KAY THOMPSON'S ELOISE

Eloise Throws a Party!

STORY BY **Lisa McClatchy**

ILLUSTRATED BY **Tammie Lyon**

Ready-to-Read
Aladdin
NEW YORK · LONDON · TORONTO · SYDNEY

ALADDIN PAPERBACKS
An imprint of Simon & Schuster Children's Publishing Division
1230 Avenue of the Americas, New York, NY 10020
Copyright © 2008 by the Estate of Kay Thompson
The text of this book was set in Century Old Style.
Manufactured in the United States of America
First Aladdin Paperbacks edition May 2008
2 4 6 8 10 9 7 5 3 1
Library of Congress Control Number 2007938994
ISBN-13: 978-1-4169-6172-7
ISBN-10: 1-4169-6172-0

My name is Eloise.
I am a city child.

I have a dog.

He is a pug.

His name is Weenie.
Today is Weenie's birthday.

I have a big
surprise for Weenie.
I am throwing him a party!

Nanny is helping me
surprise Weenie.

"Oh Nanny!" I say.
"Weenie and I are
    going for our walk now!"

I give Nanny a big wink.
She gives me the A-OK.

Weenie and I walk to Central Park.

We say hello to all
our horse friends.

Weenie sniffs the flowers.
I pick him a bouquet.

When we get back,
the manager says,
Happy birthday, Weenie!"

He hands me a box.
"For Weenie," he whispers
to me.

I give him the A-OK.

When we get to
our apartment,

Nanny yells,
"Surprise, Weenie!"
I yell,
"Surprise, Weenie!"

Room Service yells,
"Surprise, Weenie!"

The doorman yells,
"Surprise, Weenie!"

The dogs bark,
"Surprise, Weenie!"

"Look, Weenie," I say.

"And Spot, the
firemen's dalmatian!
And Priscilla
Poodle!"

'And Doxy,
the manager's
dachshund!"

We all dance around.

Then Weenie and his friends
gobble up doggy biscuits
and bonbons.

Weenie tries to eat the candles on his doggy cake.

He plays
tug-of-war

with his new
doggy toy.

I help Weenie
open his presents.
Weenie plays with
more doggy toys!

Then I give
Weenie my present.

"It is a sweater, Weenie,"
I say.

Then we all curl up
on my bed

and take a good,
long doggy nap.

Oh, I love, love,
love birthdays!